The Great Horse of Troy

by
Andrew Matthews

Illustrations by Richard Morgan

W

FRANKLIN WATTS

NEW YORK•LONDON•SYDNEY

1

Klito

Klito leaned against the rampart of the earth wall, gazing out across the plain to where Troy stood on its hill. The city's walls and rooftops shimmered in the morning heat, as though they were made of water. At any moment, it seemed Troy would shiver and burst like a bubble.

Behind Klito was the Greek camp, row after row of goat-hair tents like the one he lived in, and here and there the silk tents of the kings and princes, their banners hanging limp in the still air. Beyond the tents lay the sea, blue-green and calm, with a long line of Greek ships drawn up along its shore. The camp was the only home Klito had known – it was his world.

Klito heard a sound, turned and came face to face with Glaukos. Glaukos was

ten, the same age as
Klito, but bigger and
stronger. Klito
nodded in greeting
and received a
scowl in return.

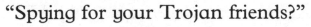

"What are
you doing here,
Trojan?" Glaukos asked.
"Spying for your Trojan friends?"

"I'm not a spy!" said Klito. "And I'm
not a Trojan. I'm Greek, like you."

Glaukos curled
his top lip in
a sneer.

"You're
no Greek!"
he said.
"Your
mother is a
Trojan, and she's a spy as well!"

"She isn't a spy!" Klito said hotly. He
could feel his anger rising, and
knew that before long he must
fight or cry.

"She's a spy, and
a slave,

and a dirty Trojan!" said Glaukos.

Klito lunged, intending to wrestle with Glaukos, but Glaukos was too quick for him. He swerved aside and stuck out his right foot so that Klito tumbled over it. Klito tried to get up, but Glaukos sent him sprawling again, with a well-aimed kick in the backside.

"You're not worth fighting, Trojan!" jeered Glaukos as he walked off, laughing.

Klito sat up, tears of rage and shame making tracks through the dust on his face.

"I'll show you!" he shouted. "I'm as good a Greek as you are, any day!"

But most of what Glaukos had said was true. Though Klito thought of himself as a Greek, he had been born a Trojan. His mother, Thetis, had been captured when he was a baby, by Greek soldiers raiding a village to the south of the city. They had taken her back to the camp and given her to a young soldier, Diodorus, to be his slave. Before long, Diodorus had fallen in love with Thetis, married her and adopted Klito as his son. Klito knew nothing about his real father. Diodorus was the only father he wanted.

Most of the people in the camp came to accept Thetis and Klito but some, like Glaukos, still looked on them as outsiders. More than anything else, Klito wanted to prove that he belonged.

"And I will!" he promised himself as he wiped the tears from his face.

"I'll show you, Glaukos. You'll see. I'll show everybody!"

At sunset, when Diodorus returned
to the tent, Thetis and Klito helped him to
unstrap his armour. Diodorus was
unusually quiet, and something about the

grim set of his mouth made Thetis ask, "Is anything wrong?"

"There's going to be an attack on the Scaean Gate tomorrow," Diodorus told her. "Lord Achilles will lead it."

"I wish I was a soldier!" said Klito. "I'd fight by your side and kill as many Trojans as I could!"

Diodorus smiled and ruffled Klito's hair.

"War is not for children," he said. "You'll have to wait a few years yet, little lion cub."

Normally, Klito liked it when Diodorus called him 'little lion cub', but this time it irritated him. If he fought against the

Trojans, it would be proof that he was a real Greek, and he could not bear to wait years. He wanted to prove himself now – right away.

2

Dead Heroes

The Greek army marched out of camp at
daybreak, before the sun was clear of the
horizon. Klito stood in the crowd that saw
the men off, cheering with the others as
the great heroes passed. First came
Achilles, staring straight ahead as his

chariot rumbled by. It was said that his armour had been forged by Hephaestos, the smith of the gods, and it glowed eerily in the dawn light. After Achilles came Odysseus, King of Ithaca, a man whose hair and beard were as red as a fox's coat. He smiled at the crowd, but his eyes were dark and brooding. Then Ajax, a golden-

haired giant, handsome as a god, but as
impatient and sulky as a small child. He
waved to the crowd, laughing excitedly,
as though the coming battle were no more
than a game.

Behind the heroes marched row after
row of soldiers. Klito saw Diodorus, an
ox-hide shield strapped to his left arm and

a war-spear clutched in his right hand.
Klito called out Diodorus's name, but
Diodorus did not turn his head.

When the last soldier had gone,
and the camp gates
slammed shut, three
crows flew up off the
ramparts of the earth
wall and followed
the army, croaking
loudly. The sound
made Klito
shiver. Crows
were corpse-
eaters, who
pecked the
eyes out of
the dead and
dying. Seeing
them was a

bad omen, and
Klito spat on
the ground
for luck.

He wandered
back to the
tent and found
Thetis outside,
sharpening a knife on a stone.

"I saw Father leave!" he said.

Thetis made no reply.

Klito said, "I wish I could have gone
with him."

Thetis looked
up from the stone.

"Thank the
gods you didn't!"
she said. "Having
a husband in
battle is worry

enough. Now, be a good boy and make
yourself useful. Take the pitcher down to the
stream and fetch me some fresh water."

Klito picked up the pitcher, then paused
and said, "What do you think would
happen to us if Father . . . I mean, if he
didn't come back?"

Thetis shook her head as if she were
trying to shake the thought away.

"You mustn't speak of such things," she
said. "Just pray that he returns safely."

All day rumours ran through the camp, as they always did when there was a battle. Some said that the army had broken through the Scaean Gate and entered Troy, others said that the Greeks had been beaten back. Klito climbed up onto the wall to try and see what was happening, but it was impossible to tell. A cloud of dust hung over the battlefield. Occasionally it lifted, so that Klito caught a glimpse of a dark mass of soldiers, or a

glint of sunshine on a sword blade, then
the dust swirled back and he could see
nothing. A breeze carried the faint sounds
of fighting to his ears – the clattering
of weapons and the screaming of men
and horses.

The battle stories the soldiers
told around the camp fires at
night made war
seem noble.
But from the
earth wall, war
looked dusty,
desperate and
confused.
Diodorus came
back at dusk, pale
and exhausted, his
shield bristling
with broken

Trojan arrows. Thetis and Klito threw
their arms around him, but Diodorus
stayed stiff and did not return their hugs.

"Lord Achilles is dead," he said. "He
was shot by a Trojan archer. Odysseus
and Ajax had to fight off thirty men to
reach his body."

Klito was astonished. 'But Achilles can't be killed!" he exclaimed. "His mother dipped him into the river Styx when he was a baby, to keep him from all harm."

"Stories, Klito, just stories," Diodorus said. "Achilles was a brave man, but he was only a man."

He laughed bitterly. "Now Odysseus and Ajax are squabbling over who should have his armour. They've asked King Agamemnon to decide."

"Shouldn't the armour be given to the bravest fighter?" Klito asked.

"The argument isn't about courage,

Klito, it's about pride," said Diodorus. "Achilles was the best of us, and now he's gone. This is a dark day for the Greeks."

Diodorus did not know it, but darker days were to follow.

Three nights after the death of Achilles, his body was burned on the beach. Klito and Diodorus joined the huge crowd that had gathered to pay its respects, and watched in silence as the flames from the

pyre rose into the night. When the fire began to die, King Agamemnon, commander-in-chief of the Greek army, stepped forward. His hooked nose and bushy eye-brows made him look proud and cruel, more like an eagle than a man.

"Achilles was a hero," he declared, "and we must honour his memory. His armour, which he wore so bravely in battle, will be awarded to his equal in courage – King Odysseus."

The crowd gasped. All eyes turned to

Ajax, to see how he would react. Ajax said nothing. He turned and walked away, the crowd parting for him. He passed close to where Klito was standing, close enough for Klito to see the shame and fury in his eyes. They were the eyes of a man who could scarcely keep control of himself.

Klito heard Diodorus murmur, "No

good will come of this."

And Diodorus was right, for next morning the camp woke to the news that Ajax was dead. Unable to bear the humiliation of being judged less courageous than Odysseus, Ajax had plunged a sword into his own heart.

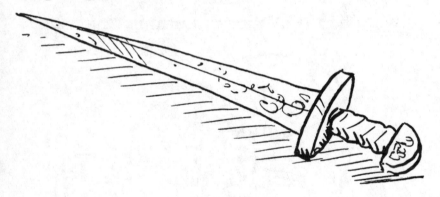

3

The Smile of Odysseus

King Agamemnon declared a truce with
King Priam of Troy, claiming that the
Greeks needed time to mourn their dead,
but the truth was that the Greek army had
lost its fighting spirit. The death of Ajax
cast a deep gloom over the camp, and

Klito overheard soldiers talking in a way that they never had before. They said that Ajax had been driven mad by the gods, as

a sign to the Greeks that their cause was unjust. Without the approval of the gods, the war with Troy could not be won.

"And why are we fighting, eh?" Klito heard a battle-scarred veteran say to Diodorus. "Because Menelaos of Sparta's wife ran off with Prince Paris of Troy! Why should thousands die because of an unfaithful wife?"

"This war was started by the pride of kings," Diodorus said. "Kings began it, and kings will decide when it ends."

"Hah!" said the veteran. "And in the meantime, the soldiers go on dying! I tell you, Diodorus, the day is coming when the men will refuse to fight, and what then, eh? How can kings make war without armies?"

Klito was dismayed. He had grown up believing that the Greeks would win the war. It had never occurred to him

that they might give up. "They can't!" he thought. "Not before I've had a chance to prove that I'm a true Greek. It's not fair!"

One morning, the Greek army was ordered to assemble on the beach to hear important news. Many people from the camp went to listen, Klito among them. He saw King Agamemnon, standing high on the prow of a beached ship, with Odysseus at his side.

"Soldiers of Greece!" Agamemnon said. "The war with Troy is over. Make

yourselves and your families ready to sail in five days' time. The camp will be struck, and what we cannot carry must be burned."

Some soldiers cheered, some wept, most stood in stunned silence.

Then Odysseus spoke. "I want every man who can use a saw and hammer to meet me outside my tent at noon," he said. "We are going to build a great wooden horse, and leave it outside Troy as

an offering to the
goddess Athene.
If she accepts the
gift, she will give us
fair weather for
our voyage."

And he
smiled. Klito
could hardly
believe it, but
Odysseus actually smiled!

That evening, in the tent, Diodorus
explained the reason for Odysseus's smile,
after making Thetis and Klito swear an
oath of secrecy. "What Agamemnon said
this morning was a lie, told to mislead any
Trojan spies," he said.

"So the army isn't leaving!" said Klito.

"The Trojans will think so," Diodorus
told him. "The ships will sail before dawn,

but once they're out of sight of land, they
will turn around and wait for nightfall.
Then they will sail back. The army will
land, cross the plain and take the city."

Klito frowned. "How?" he said.

"Odysseus's wooden horse," said
Diodorus. "Thirty men will be hidden
inside it. Odysseus believes that the
Trojans will drag the horse through the
streets in a victory parade – it
will even have
wheels to help
them move it. When
the city is asleep, the
men will come out of
the horse and open the
city gates to let
our army in."
Diodorus
paused and

grinned proudly. "I'm telling you this because when you leave with the ships, I won't be with you. I've been chosen to be one of the thirty. It's a great honour."

"A great risk, more like!" Thetis said.

"It's our only chance," said Diodorus. "We're gambling that Odysseus's cunning will give us what fighting has failed to bring – victory."

An idea came to Klito so suddenly that he almost cried out.

"Of course!" he thought. "It's perfect!"

He smiled to himself, a thin, crafty smile: the smile of Odysseus.

4

The Burning City

The atmosphere in the camp became
frantic. People scurried back and forth,
building great piles of unwanted
possessions, and all the time, by day
and by night, the hammering and
sawing went on.

Klito spent
many hours with
the men who were
building the wooden
horse. He helped
them stack wood,
and ran errands for
them until he was
accepted as one of the workers. He

watched the horse
grow from its
wheeled base. At
first it was just a
skeleton
of crisscrossing
beams, but
as the outer
planks
were
nailed

into place, a shape emerged: a warhorse
with flared nostrils and a stiff mane,
its neck proudly arched – a horse fit
for the gods.

As evening fell on the fifth day, people went down to the beach to be near the ships. Diodorus had been with Odysseus

since early morning, and Thetis was worried about him. She sat hugging her knees, staring at the sea. Klito lay on a blanket and pretended to doze, but after a while he sat up and stretched.

"I'm going for a walk," he said.

"Where?" Thetis asked.

"To look around the camp for the last time," said Klito.

Thetis looked unhappy but said, "Don't be too long Klito. We sail on the next tide."

The camp was sad, full of ghosts and memories. Part of Klito wanted to cry, but he was too excited to give in to tears. When he reached the wooden horse, he looked around. There was no one in sight;

the workmen had gone down to the beach. Klito stepped onto the base of the horse and peered up at its belly. There was a gap in the planking that would be nailed shut once the soldiers were inside. Klito clambered up the left foreleg of the horse, grasped the edge of the gap and hauled himself in.

Darkness swallowed him, but he had followed the building of the horse so closely that he knew exactly where he was. He made his way to the front section, climbed the

beams of the horse's neck, and wriggled into the small space inside its head. It was a tight fit, splintery and uncomfortable, but Klito did not mind. It would be worth it to take part in the final attack on Troy. No one would ever call him 'dirty Trojan' again.

Despite his aching limbs and the

throbbing of the splinters in his fingers, Klito managed to fall asleep.

The sound of the soldiers climbing into the horse woke him. It was too dark to see anything, but he heard whispering, and then hammering as the last planks were nailed into place. The horse lurched

forwards, and Klito had to hang on tight to keep from being thrown from his hiding

place. There was so
much bumping, creaking
and groaning that he
was sure the
horse would be
shaken to pieces.
After what seemed
like hours, the
bumping stopped.

   There was
nothing for Klito to
do but wait. Time
stretched out until it seemed
that morning would never come, but
gradually the darkness thinned to grey,
then dusty beams of sunlight shone
through the gaps in the planking. Klito felt
the dust tickle his nose, and he sneezed.

   Below him, someone swore. Strong
hands clamped around his ankles and

dragged him down. Klito looked up and
saw the face of Odysseus.

"Who are you, boy?" Odysseus hissed.

A voice said, "He's a spy! Kill him!"

Then Klito heard Diodorus say, "He's
my son."

Odysseus glared at Diodorus.

"What is he doing here? Is he mad?"

"I – I wanted to be with my father," Klito said miserably. "I wanted to help fight the Trojans, to show that I'm a true Greek."

Odysseus was red with fury. "Get him out of here!" he said.

"Too late, my lord," someone said. "The Trojans are opening the gates."

"Then go to your father, boy," Odysseus growled. "But not a sound, understand? If I hear you speak so much as a word, I shall slit your throat."

Klito made his way to Diodorus's side. Diodorus did not have to say anything; the look in his eyes was enough to make Klito feel foolish

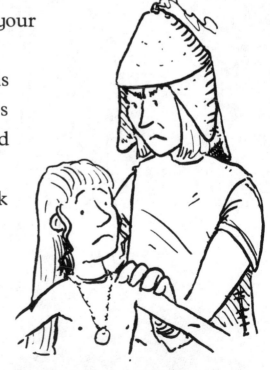

and ashamed.

The soldiers waited quietly in the stifling heat. Their tunics were soaked through with sweat, but no one groaned or complained. The silence in the horse was thick, and smelled sourly of fear.

Then the horse moved. Klito heard cheering and laughter, and felt afraid. All day, Troy celebrated. People left

garlands of flowers at the horse's feet, and
stood in its shadow to make speeches
about the courage of the Trojan army.
The city became drunk, first on victory,
then on wine.

Klito was terrified. What if the Trojans
piled wood around the horse and burned
it? He wished he were safe aboard a ship
with Thetis. He wished he could be

anywhere but where he was.

Night fell. The last drunken revellers left the square where the horse stood, and there was silence.

It was the worst wait of all. Klito's heart was thumping so loudly that he was afraid it would wake the whole city.

"Now!" hissed Odysseus.

Diodorus put his lips to Klito's ear. "Stay close to me," he said. It was all he had time to say.

The soldiers kicked out the floor planks and dropped down from the horse into the cool night air. They moved quickly through the darkened streets, killing anyone they

met. There was nothing glorious in the
killing, it was cold, quick and ruthless,
and made Klito feel sick.

Diodorus was with the soldiers who
opened the Scaean Gate. As soon as the
gate swung back, Greek soldiers poured in.

Diodorus put his hand on Klito's
shoulder and pushed him. "Go to the
beach," he said. "Run!"

"Can't I stay with you?" Klito pleaded. Diodorus's eyes hardened.

"Haven't you seen enough?" he said. "Do you want to watch women and children being butchered, because that's what will happen here tonight. Go!"

Klito ran, slowly at first, then more

quickly when he heard the screaming
begin. It was like a nightmare. In the
distance was the sea, shining silver in the
light of the moon, calm and beautiful;
from behind him came the sounds of terror
and death. He glanced over his shoulder,
and saw a thick pillar of smoke rising from
Troy. Flames were licking around the
rooftops. Klito smelled smoke and blood
on the wind. He did not look at the city

again. He ran sobbing, with his hands
pressed to his ears.

Three weeks later, Klito, Diodorus and
Thetis boarded a ship bound for Greece.
Klito and Diodorus had said nothing
about the dreadful night in Troy, but the
ship was too small for secrets.
One afternoon when Klito was on deck,
watching dolphins leap and play as they

followed the ship, Diodorus came to stand beside him.

"Well, son," Diodorus said gently, "you wanted to show everyone that you were a true Greek, and you did. How does it feel?"

"I don't know," Klito said. "I thought I would feel proud, but after what I saw in Troy . . ."

"War is cruel and terrible," said Diodorus. "It makes men mad. Your mother and I have decided to go back to my father's farm and set up home there. I want to forget the horrors of war, and that I was ever a soldier. Do you think you'll enjoy being a farmer's son?"

Klito had wanted to be a Greek, had wanted to belong. Now he saw that he

always had belonged, with Thetis and
Diodorus. They were his family.

"Yes, Father," he said.

Notes

Helen of Troy

The legend of Helen of Troy tells of how Helen, the
most beautiful woman in the world, was wooed by
many of the kings of Greece, including Odysseus of
Ithaca. She chose Melenaos, King of Sparta to be
her husband. Menelaos was the brother of
Agamemnon, the king of Mycenae, the most
powerful ruler in Greece.

Helen and Menelaos were happy together,

 until they were
visited by Prince
Paris of Troy.
Paris and Helen
fell in love, and
ran away together
to Troy. Menelaos
begged King

Priam of Troy to send Helen back to Sparta, but Priam refused. Menelaos asked his brother for help, and Agamemnon called on his allies to raise an army for a war against Troy.

Homer

The story of the Trojan War was most famously told by the Greek poet Homer, who composed his epic poem, *The Iliad*, around 750-650 BC. Homer composed another great work, *The Odyssey*. This tells of the

adventures of King Odysseus on his journey home from Troy – a voyage that took ten years.

The Ancient City of Troy

The city of Troy was a real place, though its exact location was forgotten for many centuries. Remains of the ancient city were finally uncovered at Hissarlik in Turkey by the German archaeologist Heinrich Schliemann in the 1870s. He found that the city had been rebuilt many times, and that each

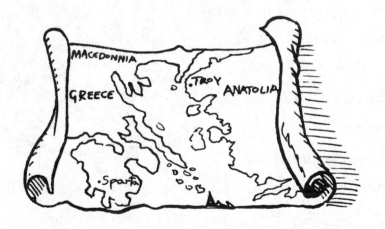

new city was built on the remains of the one before. Schliemann could not be sure which of the remains was the Troy attacked by the Greeks. Later archaeologists now consider that the remains

known as Troy VI are most likely to be the legendary city. These date from around 1250 BC. Evidence shows that the city was badly damaged by fire and an earthquake.

Bronze Age soldier

The Trojan War took place in the Bronze Age. No one knows exactly what kind of armour the soldiers wore, but it was probably similar to the armour worn later by the Greek soldiers who were known as 'Hoplites'. It consisted of a shield, a helmet, a breastplate and leg-covers called 'greaves', and would have weighed approximately 32 kilogrammes.

63

Sparks: Historical Adventures